THE PENGUIN POETS

HOLD FAST

Dennis Silk was born in 1928 in London. In 1955 he emigrated to Jerusalem, where he has lived ever since. His poetry has appeared in a number of collections published in London and Jerusalem, in a small-press book published in Massachusetts in 1964, in many journals and reviews, and in *The Punished Land*, which is also available from Penguin Books.

HOLD FAST

Poems by

DENNIS SILK

Elisabeth Sifton Books
PENGUIN BOOKS

ELISABETH SIFTON BOOKS · PENGUIN BOOKS

Viking Penguin Inc., 40 West 23rd Street,
New York, New York 10010, U.S.A.
Penguin Books Ltd, Harmondsworth,
Middlesex, England
Penguin Books Australia Ltd, Ringwood,
Victoria, Australia
Penguin Books Canada Limited, 2801 John Street,
Markham, Ontario, Canada L3R IB4
Penguin Books (N.Z.) Ltd, 182–190 Wairau Road,
Auckland 10, New Zealand

First published in the United States of America
in simultaneous hardcover and paperback editions
by Viking Penguin Inc. 1984
Published simultaneously in Canada

Library of Congress Catalog Card Number: 84-61110

Mickey Rabina lent me a roof in New York; Dina Recanati and the National
Foundation for Jewish Culture eased my stay there.

"Difficulties of an Actress," "Grand Central," "Pastoral of the Fast Talk-
ers," and "Memories of '57" appeared originally in *The American Poetry Re-
view;* "Self-Portrait by the Hudson River," "A big freeway sandwich," "Lots
of furniture's put out in the street," "Shamelessly he fingerprinted my face,"
and "Next" in *Forthcoming;* portions of "Guide to Jerusalem" in *The Liter-
ary Review;* and "Kidney-isle" in *Stand.*

Grateful acknowledgment is made to Atheneum Publishers for permission to
reprint a selection from "Questions to Tourists Stopped by a Pineapple
Field" from *Opening the Hand* by W. S. Merwin. Copyright © W. S. Mer-
win, 1983.

Printed in the United States of America by
The Murray Printing Corporation, Westford, Massachusetts
Set in Devinne

For Avigail Agranat and Adele de Cruz

Contents

᛭ Hold Fast

III OFF TO BOSTON AND NEW HAVEN

IV ENTR'ACTE

V AT LARGE

VI QUEASY

Hold Fast

"Poets like travel."
—HENRI MICHAUX

I LAFAYETTE STREET

॥

The debonair Double, a light mac over his arm, and with a
traveling bag all of whose pouches say *Good-bye,* walks
across the jetway into the plane. His semblance walks
with him. It's odd two look-alikes should look so different.
Who hands over the boarding pass? Who sits at the cabin
window as Levant softens into Acgean, Aegean winces
into North? I ... who? Now we hover above London, that
place of contraction on the globe. Semblance sighs. It's
that sulky place where he began. (For English sulks in a
night-tent in London. Asthmatic poet, advised the Dou-
ble, you need the easy breath of the Levant.)

॥

Helicopter blade, serious revolving brow of thought,
above parceled-out English fields
glad to expire so wanly.

A frittering mind revolves
in worry-cloud
and harries itself at London.

Hold fast, flashes the Double,
my mac over my left arm,
your right arm extended
above New York,
quickening toward Kennedy,
we'll see the polyps
of light,
the grid.

Thinking our way through Customs,
we'll declare all save what we came for,
which soon enough we'll know because
those valuables are speeding toward us.

凹

Over there, old chap,
teasingly says the Black
at Information.

Put on your scarf.
WALK. DON'T WALK.
Put on your scarf.

凹

A Jamaican
aims his yellow peril
at rainy light.
I arrive, we arrive—

two laughing ex-Brits
on whom the sun set—
at the loft of Avigail.

凹

A Londoner supposes a loft
a run-down aviary for an Ibsen duck.
Not so with a New York loft.
You must follow your lucky hunch
through hint and ad, you must dice for the
long floor of ex-factory space.
If you've a New York loft you've won a bunch.
You can roller-skate through waxed space
and hear the light applaud.

凹

There are linen-cupboards here and lots of towels.

The sliding glass screen for the bath delights
me and my Double.

It's an American novelty.

Lots of wall.

And fresh as paint
save that the paint here is fresh—a new co-op
has taken over the building.

We walk around, circumspect,
hands behind our back like the English curate,
me and my Double.

Benightedness of the Levant!

Welcoming Avigail is dismayed by
my shadowy side-show.

Her eyes say: *Do we have to have him?*

I shrug. She nods.
This is what it is to have friends.

Her Yuval takes me by the hand and shows me
a huge dollhouse.

Watchdog Double must think it's a kennel
because he gets into it on all fours,
curls up, and soon is snoring disagreeably.

And this is his first night in New York.

Yuval gives him an odd look
but Avigail is glad he's curled into *Away*.

ﺟﻞ

She asks about Jerusalem
and our friends, there,
in the loony capital,
and the loops they loop, there,

and my snoring friend,
does he have a name,
will he be nice to Yuval,
shall we cut keys for him,
will he be always
the sharer of my life?

𖤐

Yes, I say, we've set up house there, Double and me, in the
Levant. Of course, that's a misnomer. For we live in the
punished land. Those useless old maps have nice names:
The Trucial States, Palestine. I'd like to run up the flag of
then. If its colors weren't spiteful, if they blended without
blur or worse but

𖤐

She puts Yuval to bed
in the New World. Pillow-song
sweetens the loft.

Double and Yuval sleep
and at her Lafayette window
we study the white code of steam
from street-vents.

I've not seen such vents of steam before
that are so American and ordinary
and daisy up through asphalt.

And from the printer opposite the steam
and the entire way to Palo Alto
it will be my study.

Maybe the Double can decode it for me,
who fills the dollhouse with such ugliness.
Sometimes he's so debonair, other times so gloomy,

he's the Double of a Double,
I don't latch on to him,
he's fly-catcher Harlequin and frowning Doctor,
he must have a reversible mac.

凹

Oddly I slip
through interstices
of myself into the hands
of the Other.

I room with him
because he reads this Indian sign language.

凹

I'll buy myself a watch and some power,
ginseng or high-stepping boot,
a conversion table.

A tiniest homunculus, New York,
tries out his arms freely
in your coat.

II SERIOUS KITCHENS

꿻

With orange juice, Sunnysides-up and bacon,
with ritual grub,
I install myself on the West Side.

II

I take my many-buttoned shirt to the cleaners,
and it comes back Hudson color.
Or I worry my way through the thrift shop,
looking for a belt to hold up my self-respect,
or a beret in chancy May.

I recall reading
about a caliph who liked his vizier so much
he had one suit sewn for the two of them.
It was a capacious though subtle affair.
Anyway, it would have been dangerous to laugh
at what these two did.

꿻

A big freeway sandwich
teaches the art of chewing.
This fast food from Brooklyn
is digested on the West Side.

In a mysterious
duplication, hands
that began service in Brooklyn
catch me the whizzing West Side cake.

〰 Hat Trick

You need a good eye to pick out
from the moving rack of clothes
anyone's shirt and jacket.
He picks out my things very well.
Moreover, he wraps them for me
in chancy May
raining on the town and my hat.

I've no routine for the entire town
but am juggler enough
to wear my hat on the cleaned sleeve
of my jacket

or place it
on a right chair in Manhattan
where it won't be sad
or sadden.

〰 Primitive

With the ferrule she
inscribed that pavement-circle
he abetted—he stepped inside
that happy diagram. Moreover,
she had the earrings
of a tribal person.

They'd go to Vermont ten days, drive through
unsmudged mountain.

彐 Amsterdam Avenue

Braided hairdo of the day, completed
with a threat of beads.
Petulance of an unhappy gamester.

Botanica del Carmen, endow
the sidewalk with incense.

II PURCHASE

I vaguely bought this pineapple
and did not learn its lingo.

Yet when I slice off its top-knot
of a true Carib
it pleads with me

¿Habla español?
You'll try? T'anks.

彐 Mugger

That unabashed street-person
in the overdressed inner hallway he penetrated—
below peeling angels and unnecessary half-columns,
to the side of the service lift with its brushes and buckets—
that spooky person took me by the windpipe.

止

Lots of furniture's put out in the street
I can move into this poem.

Moreover,
I begin to get the notion of the grid here.
96th Street, 97th, that's clear enough
even to my name-loving self.
Lexington and 92nd—
coordinates of an artillery man.
Cannon trained along these avenues
discharge spinach pie and doughnut.

II

Lots of phones put themselves out
to move me out of my poem.
I do up my fly and answer
the softly clamorous, the democratic.

There's a rain of doughnut in my mind.

I must be pliable yet persistent
and more delicate than pie crust.

止

Encounter
of shoeshine man and shoe, Kung Fu
graffiti midnight boys transmit, under-
water surprising bus ride, newspaper
of my intimate spook, food
too fast to eat.

II

Man extends his foot
in profile, and shoeshine man
accepts that Chinese shadow—
NY wants you to travel light.

III OFF TO BOSTON
AND NEW HAVEN

卍

Friends show me the frame houses of New England
where the daemon must live.

I am a transient in these towns
and need quick glue.

卍

Strapping on my book,
I think of Bashō
and his trudged circuit of poems.

Is this a purse?
No, it is a pouch of my traveling bag.
Is this a person?

卍

The Double is the shadow kids paint on walls there,
he's the spooky reassurance,
the mugger who stole from himself
and felt so embarrassed.

ᴫ Saint-Gaudens' *The Union Dead*

Maybe that regiment could retrieve
the cantankerous Semites,
drumming through Palestine
rescue the smithereens.

II

Just a little softer,
please.
More groves, less graves.
If Palestine were more Latin . . .

if it were more Latin
it would not be Palestine.

凵 Difficulties of an Actress

Two wise men of Jerusalem, two teachers of yours—
a Dr. Coppelius and a Dr. Caligari—
plot in New York, over breakfast,
their lively stroll on the East Side.

These wisest of the charlatans
consider a basketball net's long shadow,
and a hoist going up, and a hard-hat worker
framed by and declaiming among timber,
till brandy of the street works on them.

And they are more guileless than you may guess,
and don't entrap a single young person,
neither you nor any young person,
or hocus you into an Olympia
of clockwork sighs and *Ohs*.

II

Here's a tricked charlatan
who got caught in his cape
to free you.

You might thank him.

Thankyou and *Thankyou* and once again *Thankyou*.

And the new teacher?

Your shadow on the sidewalk.

Now the *khamseen* lifts,
you and you
walk through five o'clock light.
You talk it over with your spook
in a quiet suburb.

III

The head *kaput*.

Not a comedian to tease sleepyhead.

Theatre is anodyne,
there,
and aims shift as subscribers
in sleep or as they shift
in pushed-down and warded-off townships.

Will you be one of the broken women,
I wonder,
on that theatre-wheel, there,
playing anecdotes for the smiling accomplice?

(How much he likes his fourth wall and his anecdote.)

But tonight he's not pleased.

The play is crisscrossed
by considerations he finds odd.

This actress about to betray her husband
entirely forgets the assignation
because the throb of her pulse fascinates her,
and she sits down to stare at her wrist.

The play has shaken off its anecdote.

Or as she prepares her jump from the balcony
this actress climbs into the third person, observes:
Now she is about to jump from the balcony.

Such interruptions do not please the fourth-wall person.

Now she and her lover consider the angle
a door makes with its frame,
how are they to dispose of her husband?

The Double has set fire to the anecdote
in the interest of heaven.

The actress is smoke but saved.

Yet the Double is not a safety match.

V AT LARGE

凹

Kidney-isle
examined by Dr. Plane.
Cotton-wool altitude now.

I eat whisked things only.
Cloud sits at my plate.

Some of this cloud
reminds me of smoke rings
a Hebrew poet blew
in Bucharest or Tel Aviv.

I am at large,
an interstate
kidnapper of your attention.

凹 Los Angeles

Latitude of Tel Aviv
but opulent opulent.
Someone must have dug up a Levant root
and planted it here.

All the palms talk one Semitic lingo or another.
At UCLA it's Accadian.
Uptown it has a more Babylonish sound.
Anyway, they clearly didn't start here.

I have said to the philodendron *You
are my mother and my brother*
and to the magnolia
I take off my hat to you.

山

If I were wearing a hat
I couldn't tip it for Mississippi
for it's the wrong side of the plane
(I am the golem of an aviator).

Nor could I make my hat into a raft
or endow the river with a pleasure boat.
But if this wing were a paddle wheel,
it would stir the river.
                    Hat and wheel,

I've bartered you for a wing
that has killed arrival and departure.

山

A joker and a schoolmaster redouble
their effort to seduce me across the tracks
of southern California.

It's hard to know who really wears the trousers.

Schoolmaster wears left trouser, joker the right.
One wears a black suspender, one a white.
They wear two black two white in most ranchhouses.

It is the joker I—*I?*—like best.
The schoolmaster will conduct the inquest.

凵 Lounge

Who are all these patient people
in B or C
I frequent with the Double?

He points them out to me.
They are waiting for San Francisco
in the fetal lounge,
drinking from an Air California cup
some liquid.

I stupefy my Double with Happy Landing.
What will become of him?

凵

Funny to peel into candy
and laughter.
The skins of me are not in some worried lounge.

I have a liking for mirrors
where Dennis is laughing.

𝕁 Wardrobe

Lots of shirts and under cellophane
the mover.
This shirt buys me. I want to be bought.

It costs twenty-two dollars
and has six outstanding buttons.
It's shirt-blue not Pacific blue.

II

My hat is in the East. And I'm on the West Coast.

But my many-buttoned shirt gives me security
and I live in it as in the house of the poem.

III

A friend
wears the brother of my blue shirt
in brown.

IV

I buy myself Jockey Classic briefs
because Pegasus is a curt horse.

𝕁 Rain: Gratitude

First umbrella
in California.

With my cardigan
I cover the philodendron
that covered me.

凷 Kitchen

I considered the Pacific through a serviette-ring
because California caressed me out of the angular.

凷 Chinatown, San Francisco

Herbarium? Aquarium?
I don't know what name to give this shop.
And these Chinese are reluctant with Caucasians
to say much.

Calmed-down shark fin, herb of fish—
it's a kind of sea-garden of the Chinese.
They hold on with coolie strength to their kitchen.

I've fallen into their streets.
I've the pleasure of a stranger among gutturals
of these determined people.
Sound of a bat connecting with a ball
their language.

II

The trolley-girl calls out a melancholy word for dumpling
at the Dim Sum restaurant.
They order well.
Steamed bun of pork at breakfast
and twice-cooked pork—
it's hard to learn the sound of their dishes—
these are the little city meats they eat here.

There's a Brechtian sense of the dollar here.
Girl pushing trolley won't be ransomed
as in doll-theatre.

These are the commercial Chinese.

Not as tireless as her I swim through
plates and cups till my tide pulls me back.

III

This bun promises me double happiness
if I eat well, and all the little city meats
applaud a brief plate.
                                    I eat well.
I am the undistracted transient
of this restaurant.

IV

Chinatown flickers out at Vallejo.
At Grant Avenue they have a lion-gate
for the foreign devil to slither under.
Almost you expect Book of the Dead guards:
Who are you?

A half-flicker at Columbus
where a Vietnamese daughter and mother
draw a flimsy shop about themselves.
Careless of all, they sell Arabian bread,
Chinese egg roll, and *ful* I know from Palestine.

Their limbo is defined by fun-porno.
Here are booths to which the lonely go
and shyly savage punks I have not pondered.

A Levant mind prunes this.

V

I yesterday surprised gamblers
among dicing cups.

In mild shops gods hide.
It's hard to surprise here.

But when they lion-danced
I saw the thunder in these prudent people.
Their firecracker scorched my winter coat.

凹 Oven of Good Things

These are the little city meats
I eat in steamy cafés.

In the hermetic kitchen
noodle and nib converge.

In the night-kitchen
                              my foods
on a low flame.

凹 The Last of Stockton Street

Fortune cookies sustain me through the night of the poem.
I extract a motto:
Very soon, and in pleasant company.

I will take your Chinese faces with me,
not those boxed
masks of Peking Opera types.

凹

Three copies of this hideous film screened in one plane
suggest serial hell.

II   LIFE-BELT DRILL

This stewardess puts such vim into her dumb show
and another says *Sir* with such ardor.

凹 The Visit

The Double levitates
over Nebraska.
Snowy again.

Less levitation, more levity,
would be well for us in Chicago.
Deplane, Double.

He deplaned. The peak-capped
chief imagination of Michigan
was there to embrace us, put our bags
in the boot, drive us
to his lake home
where he had composed carefully
the score of that water.

We gave him
wind chimes tuned
to a classical Greek scale—
it was to have
Pythagoras to breakfast.

Such mathematics pleased
his debonair mind.
He essayed a chime.

It deflected
the Double spiraling out
on some dull errand,
fetched him back
to the solid breakfast of friends.

VI QUEASY

凹

Here is the twin
of the man who folded a napkin
for my last good table in Brooklyn.

Hands that pour tea
into this cup on Avenue C
are heimish and nightmarish to me.

凹

Two scoops
and it's rum-raisin all the way.

How about a glass of mango
in chancy May?
Or perhaps papaya?
How about that?

If I took one scoop,
one scoop of rum-raisin?

In the mango grass
of papaya park

they range and range
like royal deer.

One scoop.

凹 Grand Central

Toy-theatre figures
escalate down with cutout profile
and perfect in the text of the actor.

Sleepy steps dissolve. Spinach pies replenish.

(Where is the poem-crazy person?
He sips from a plastic cup, and observes.

Where is the poem-crazy person?
Among whizzing cake and projectiles.

Where is the poem-crazy person?
He stood. He dissolves.)

VII SUMMER HIT SUDDENLY

卟

Even King Kong went to the beach
and lolled and blocked all bad thoughts
jabbing at him and washed weather
in water he felt so reduced.
Summer hit suddenly.

卟

Paradoxical that the hurry-wheels
stopped. It was the Fourth of July
and they were freedom-wheels, maybe.

They stopped. Before they started
I climbed in for Brewster North,
then Pawling and a crackerless
Sunday.   Day without a tunnel,
no siren and no ether,
and the track jumps high
on the Fourth of July.

⿻ Pastoral of the Fast Talkers

For Hilda O'Connell and Adele de Cruz

The flag
of the United States, a gaudy
bird among trees,
tries out its fifty notes
at Pawling, where kids
pick up a frayed town-man
outside Noodle Palace,
and though the driver girl
brakes badly—I hate
these gear-disputes—
gratefully we arrive
at the hacienda of Hilda.

II

(A studio, actually,
housing such calculations
New York should be startled by.)

All its windows
are so pleased by green, everything
is gauche and lovesick.
It's a transparent
American arrangement.

Friends
on a stagy platform gesture to
an audience of bark—
town actors
talking to the country-people.
An Italian-seeming girl
considers me, then

31

runs back to volleyball
strange as baseball to me.
Others bend over a barbecue.

Kabuki-like I saunter over
where teams of fast talkers
play volleyball to
Hit it up Hit it up I've
got it Ro-
tate Ro- oh
how I like it in the middle
of the middle to
hit it up
tenderly over the net.
Yes, I am less
teased by this game than are old
world trees by new talkers.

The way the ball leaves my palm pleases
me, and the sharpness
of *Hit it up Hit*
it up as the light
loses confidence—surely it should
keep up appearances
for these brisk persons.

VIII FLASHBULB

⼭ Intersection Man

Loitering among streets of pencil stubs,
I see they are good for doodles.
They cannot, on their sidewalk, do well.

They erase well.

Mine behind my ear
will be the doorpost of my day
and frame those intersections where
Manhattan numbers thicken and bite.

II

I wave goodbye to myself at the jetty.

He has heartbreak, going,
whose flashbulb failed
in that wheeling car
at the intersection.

How he sulks in his cabin.

I'm at large,
clandestine in the darkroom
of some borough.

ᵭ Ventriloquist's Dummy,
   Macdougal Street

Charlie McCarthy, hinged
talker, I'll throw
into you such repartee
your first master
may pause. And I'm innocent
of wit—you elicited
words gathering
under *Can't* and
Shan't, found the chattering
teeth of poetry.

ᵭ Javanese Shadow Figures

Almond-eyed, level-voiced,
here are the princes.

They have mathematical
gradations of gold and black
for the understander.

In each play they dispatch red ogres.

The two cool brothers, in the car, at 42nd,
gold Ardjuna and Yudistira,
are ruffled by a discordant giant
who has a bottle in the paper bag
they put everything into in America.

川

Shamelessly he fingerprinted my face
and remaindered me among the ten thousand books.

A Hong Kong tailor in Mott Street
sewed back two buttons for a quarter.
I felt a spurious happiness
among the machines of the immigrant.

Poetry?
I know it isn't
where I am
but it is my overcoat.

川

At the Magic Cue Billiard Academy,
where was the opportunist of cues
who fills all pockets at once?

37 tables waited.

DON'T PLAY IF YOU CAN'T PAY the sign said.

EAT & RUN the sign said.
Did I bolt down
a too-hasty pudding?

To drive through this town
you need three wheels
and the fourth is wilfulness.

﷼

The Bronx, provoked hoopoe-bird
that flares and shits,
then Yonkers—
I've a Dutch uncle, there, who's bonkers—
we and them
on the closed car tour.

Says Eddie, over a Hennessy and Coke,
After Harlem
you'd make it in Singapore.

We picked up all the bits
from Columbia to Grand Concourse,
so it's no joke many disappeared
through the porous.

﷼ SoHo Rehearsal

"What do you know about pineapples?" he asks
(this young actor is a good one
and flicks the tourist in his silly car).
"Do you like pineapples or pineapple labels?
Do you like pineapples fresh or crushed?
Have you seen a pineapple field?"

Who has time for worldly pineapple?
I'll take juice.

⑪ Next

Houston?
No. Jerusalem.

When I was in—
did I sleep in that New Haven frame house
in Chicago, that swan boat from Charles
ferry me over the East River?

IX FINAL CALL

凹 Self-Portrait by the Hudson River

I am all eyebrow and fluidity
by the side of this serviceable river
heavy with wharves and piers.
I am volatile as a pencil
in the hand of a poet.

My expression is always changing.
Probably I vex you, Hudson.

It is quite early a.m.
and I intend to paint *me*
in a likely pose.

We have two folding chairs, I and *me*,
and the look of contestants.

Me has the frozen eyebrows
of a dubious person found in the hallway.
With his whiskers he sniffs out my purse
and expedients.

Me is the mugger.

This criminal indicates the river,
its landings and piers,
its colors to New Jersey.

Me would sit in some tracing of a town
and get his oxygen from the scaffolding
and cranes.
That is where to study him,
the great criminal.

I observe his face coming and going, there,
it's sometimes almost my own in hopeful color,
sometimes it lapses into a tracing.
It's as though an architect's drawing inhaled and exhaled.

My prepared colors cannot paint his ghost town.

Noting the helplessness of my palette
to paint *me,*
the great criminal scowls.

Not a missionary jogger intervenes
and I don't know how to conclude with this
white gentleman by the bank of the Hudson.

Guide to Jerusalem

For Leon Wieseltier

⽌ Memories of '57

We drink juice and guard oil rigs
by the river that lost heart
and became a Levant fiasco.

We unload chemicals.

We dig the beginning of a road.

In a free spell we follow water-courses.

These oilmen will sink their pipes
and not recover them.

Do you know the story of the Turkish admiral
who sailed out to bombard Gibraltar
and sailed around without finding it
and returning informed his Sultan:
Gibraltar yok (meaning Gibraltar isn't there)?

We were the feckless princes of those shacks.

꒐ Guide to Jerusalem (Third Edition)

I NEIGHBORHOOD

He lives under this holy mountain.
Time for *schloffen* he says to his friend.
Across the wadi you see his parked car
and know he and his friend are there.

II COLLEAGUE

No soap in my pocket
to wash away the handshake,
and the writer I met now,
voluble and talented,
hurries to read his article
in the morning newspaper.

III PROXY

These Muslim shopmen—they are very busy—
send their shoes to pray at the mosque.

IV PRAISE IN OCTOBER

All summer you have meddled,
old father,
and tired our poem.
Moony rain
revives the metal horse
in the playground.

V VALENTINE TO TEL AVIV

Postcard, little bike
on the thoroughfare,
did you get through?

VI SACRIFICE OF ISAAC
(*Do-it-yourself sonnet*)
monotone.
army camp.
altar stone
stomach cramp.

procurer
target-dummy.
Sarah.
mummy.

rhetoric
needless ram.
thicket
am what I am."

Moriah
paranoia.

VII HYGIENE

Better Pan
among the bougainvillea than
a rifleman.

VIII THE JEWISH SETTLEMENT IN PALESTINE

In a canoe from the nineteenth century
we meet shallows followed by cataracts
it was just like the Levant to devise.
Wearing old hats we look at naive maps,
unprepared mettlesome travelers perhaps.

⛎ Politics

On my way through our side of town,
I note vine
and caper.
Sauntering through their side of town,
I note caper
and vine.

II

We take in air like the gecko.

One mother
concedes us the air
of Palestine.

⛎ Etching Game: David Before the Ark

For Ivan Schwebel

Loners don't pass but laugh
the ball through serious legs
into the net that agrees
with them.

You've scratched your *Samuel*
thought onto the plate—
the Ark is danced
home, not a left back
closes the field, the copper
crowd clap.

Notes

LAFAYETTE STREET
Palestine. I quote from the Argument to an earlier sequence
of poems, *The Punished Land.* "She's called Palestine because
it's her best name. It's not the Palestine of the Fatah, or the
Greater Israel of the irredentists."

Avigail—Ŭvègīl.

Yuval—Yūvŭl.

ENTR'ACTE
Olympia. The automaton dancer from E. T. A. Hoffmann's
"The Sandman."

AT LARGE
"Some of this cloud . . ." Lea Goldberg's *Smoke Rings* was
published in Tel Aviv in 1935.

FLASHBULB
SoHo Rehearsal. The play was Joseph Chaikin's *Tourists &
Refugees No. 2,* and the young actor was Will Patton. The
quoted lines are from Mira Rafalowicz's text.

Next. Perhaps a transient can be forgiven for thinking that the swan boats plied the Charles River.

GUIDE TO JERUSALEM
Memories of '57. An oil mining camp near the Dead Sea.

The Jewish Settlement in Palestine. The pre-1948 "state in the making," *not* the new settlements on the West Bank.